How the Sun Got to Coco's House

To my son, Pete.
Ever an artist and
always an inspiration to me.

First U.S. edition 2015

Library of Congress Catalog Card Number 2014955416
ISBN 978-0-7636-8109-8

20 19 18 17 16 15 APS 10 9 8 7 6 5 4 3 2 1

Printed in Humen, Dongguan, China

This book was typeset in Garamond Ludlow.
The illustrations were done in ink and watercolor.

Candlewick Press
99 Dover Street
Somerville, Massachusetts 02144

visit us at www.candlewick.com

CANDLEWICK PRESS

How the Sun
Got to Coco's House

BOB GRAHAM

It had to start somewhere.

While Coco slept far away, the sun crept up slowly behind a hill, paused for a moment, and seemed to think twice . . .

before it plunged down the other side and skidded giddily across the water.

It touched a fisherman's cap and, with help from the wind . . .

blew it off!

The sun tumbled end over end.
It was caught briefly in the eye of a whale . . .

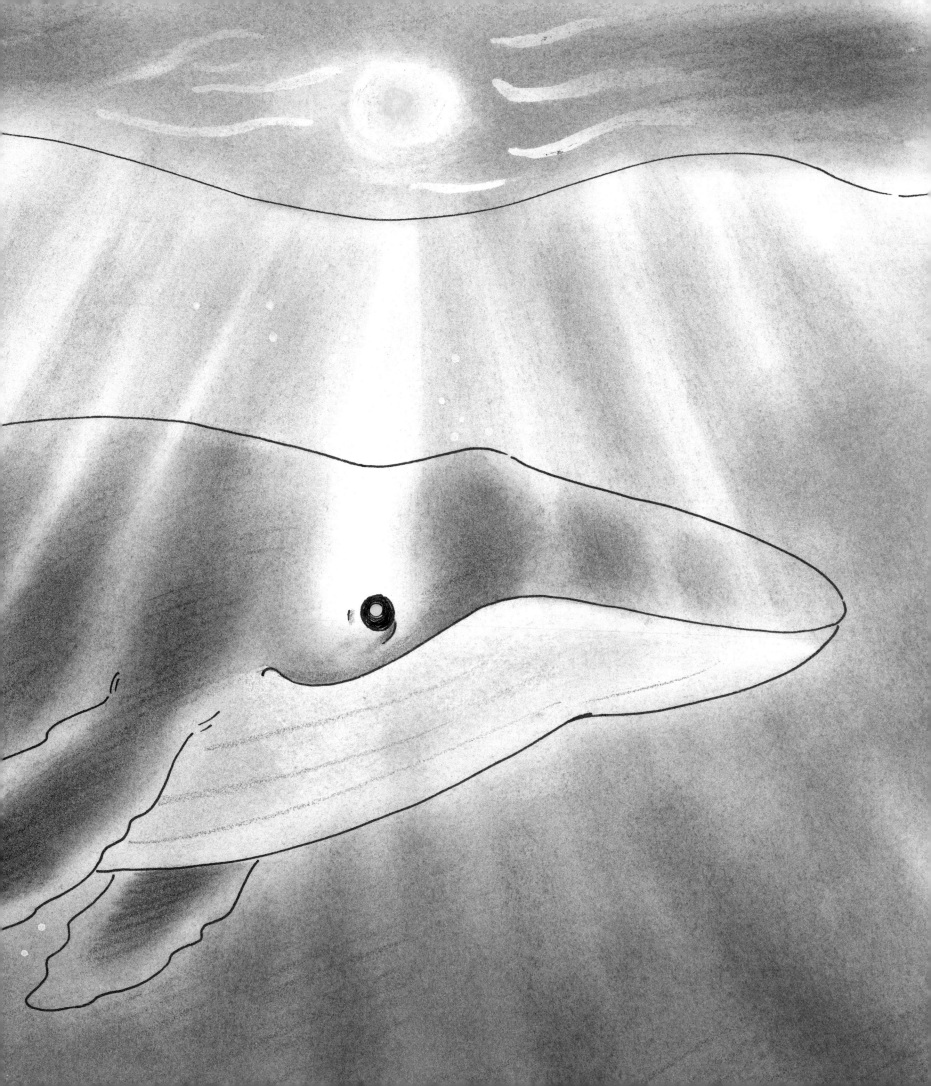

then headed up the beach

and out over frozen forests, making shadows on the snow

and in Jung Su's footsteps.

The rising sun met birds still flying south for
the winter and a plane flying high in the night.

It balanced out on the wing — just for young Lovejoy,
off to visit his grandma.

It crossed a city, took a shortcut down an alley,

and waited patiently outside an old lady's window to be let in.

The sun took off over the countryside,

woke bears

and snow cats

and caught Kosha and his father
on their way to market.

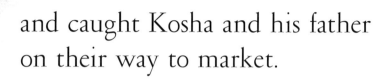

High over a desert,

it met the rain.

Over the mountains, in a small village,
Alika's toe broke ice in a puddle.

Then the sun leaped
whole countries,
chasing the night.

It lit the East Side of a city and took
passing glances at itself in office towers.

Bold as you like,
it extinguished
the streetlights
on Coco's street.

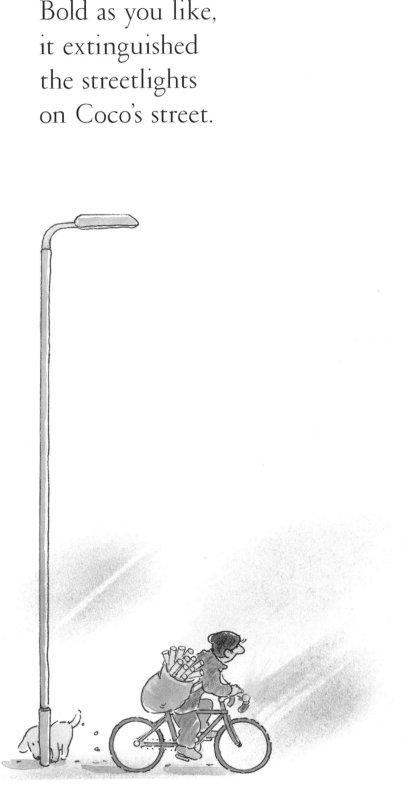

It briefly trapped itself in
the paperboy's bell.

Then . . .

the winter sun barged straight through Coco's window!

It followed her down the hall,

made itself quite at home on her mom and dad's bed,

and joined them for breakfast.

After such a dash, the sun had time on its hands. So did Coco!

So did Coco's friends!

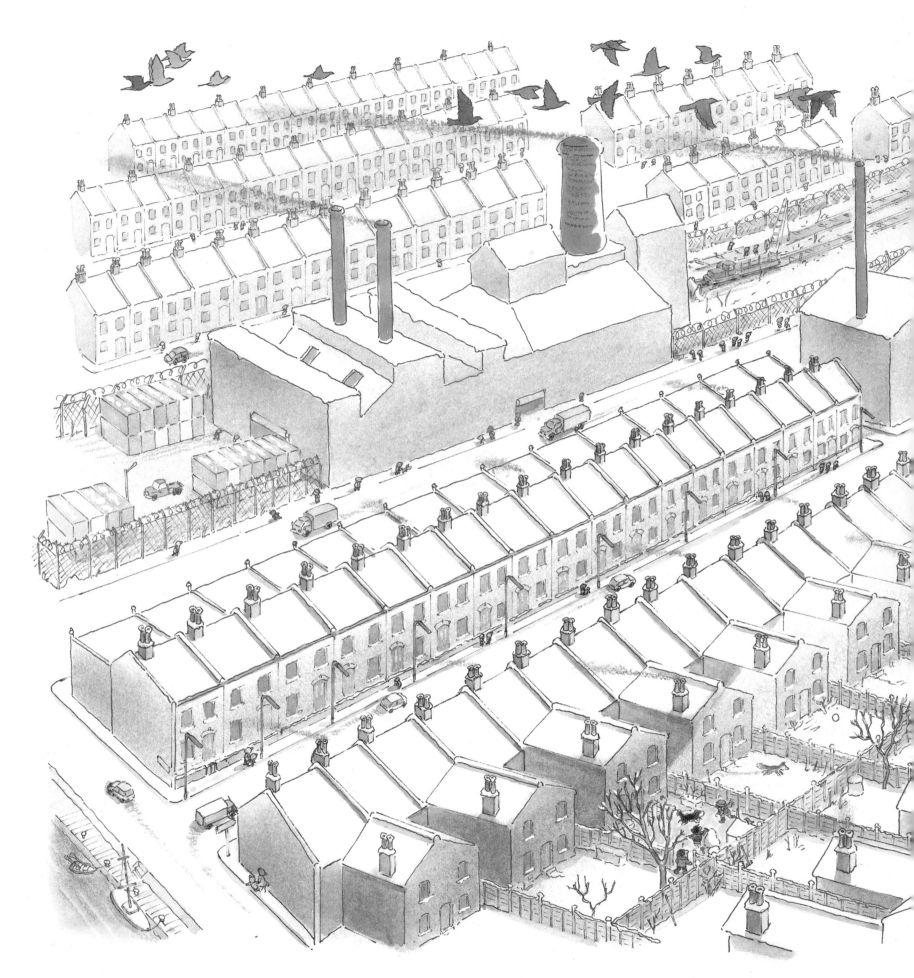

But for a few passing clouds,

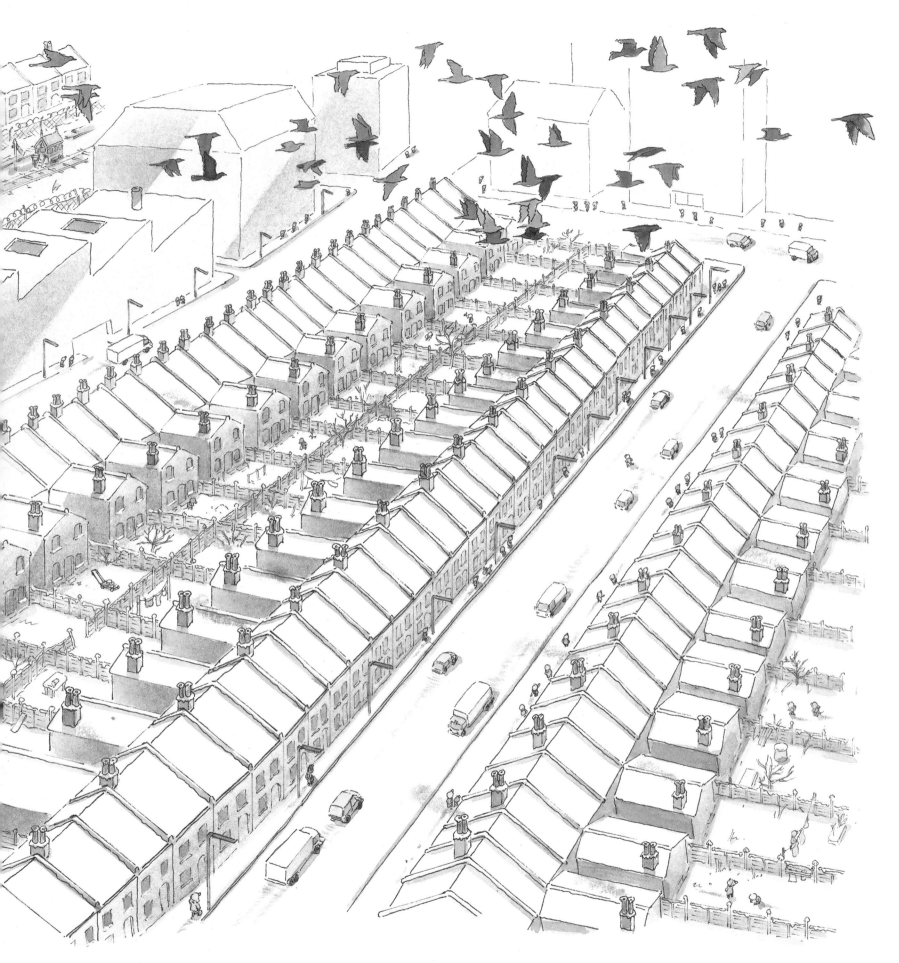

they spent the whole day together.